CAPTAIN CHEECH

by Cheech Marin

illustrated by Orlando L. Ramírez

HarperCollins*Publishers*

GOOD MORNING!

My name is Cheech, and I'll be your school bus driver today. I am a really, really, really, **REALLY** good bus driver. I always get to school on time, and I always know the **BEST** shortcuts.

One day my Cheecharrones were getting on the bus, and Carmen stopped to talk to me. "Hey, Cheech!" she said. "Did you hear about the boat race?"

"Boat race?" I asked.

"Yeah!" Moe joined in. "Vanessa and her crew challenged us to a boat race on Monday after school. We're gonna win for sure!"

"This reminds me of when I was a kid," I said. "We used to make boats out of paper and race them down a little river in the park."

"Yeah," Moe said. "This'll be just like that."

"So," Eugene said. "Cheech, I was wondering if we could maybe borrow your school bus for the weekend."

I wondered why a bunch of kids would need to borrow a school bus. I thought maybe they were going to paint a mural on the side for me. Or maybe they were going to get me a new steering wheel as a present.

I got very excited. The Cheecharrones were so nice. It wasn't even my birthday!

When I woke up Monday morning, my bus was covered with a sheet.

Eugene said, "Good morning, Cheech. Feast your eyes on the amazing . . . the magnificent . . .

"Everyone is laughing at us!" I said.
"But I know how to stop them."

Everyone stops when they see my stop sign! That's what I call a "bus stop."

When Vanessa and her friends saw the sailbus, they couldn't help but smile. "That boat is amazing!" Vanessa said. "But what if water gets in through the windows?"

"Enough talking," Moe said. "Let's start racing!

One, two, three . . .

GO!"

First
it
was
too
FISHY.

Then the fish got friendly!

Vanessa's boat was far behind. "We're gonna win for sure," Joey shouted.

But **then** the fish got **TOO** friendly.

Vanessa was gaining fast, and we were almost at the finish line!

"Cheech!" Moe screamed. "This race is too close! We've gotta do something!"

"I've got an idea," I said.

WE WON!

"What a great race!" Vanessa said. "When I grow up, I want to be a bus driver just so I can have one of those stop signs. Then I'll win all the races!"

I said, "Well, at least it's over."
"Not quite," Moe said.

To my children—Carmen, Joey, and Jasmine.
—C.M.

To all children who love the ocean, boats, adventure, and fair play.
—O.L.R.

Captain Cheech
Text copyright © 2008 by Cheech Marin
Illustrations copyright © 2008 by Orlando L. Ramírez

Library of Congress Cataloging-in-Publication Data is available.
ISBN 978-0-06-113206-3 (trade bdg.) — ISBN 978-0-06-113208-7 (lib. bdg.)

Designed by Stephanie Bart-Horvath
1 2 3 4 5 6 7 8 9 10
❖
First Edition